Mantle of the Gods:

Book 1

Mantle of Magic

By

Christopher M Delano

Prologue

My name is Martin Seelie. I am a hedge wizard. One of the last people that can use real magic and this is the story about how I became a God and returned magic to the world.

Chapter 1

My story starts on a snowy day in February. I was stuck in prison for a crime I did not commit. Just biding my until my release. Making sure no one knows that I have magic. Then the announcement happened that I was to report to the control center. There a Sergeant waiting for me.

I have your ex-wife on the phone for you.

I knew it was bad. So I followed him to his office. He sat me down and put the phone on speaker.

Mrs. Seelie I have him now.

Martin it really bad. Just tell me what happened. Cady is in the hospital. The doctors say she is not going to make it long,

What is the timeline? 2 maybe 3 days. What can I do?

Pray for Miracle. I know that you really can't do much but I wanted you to know. Keep me updated. I'll talk to you soon. The call hangs up.

Seelie do you need to call psych for you? No Sir I'll be fine. If you change your mind just one of the officers knows.

Thank you.

I head back to the block. He knocks on his neighbor's door. I need all your black paint and the biggest brush that you have. It's going to cost you. Add to my bill. Ok. He hands over the items that were requested. Martin heads into the yard which is empty except for the sleeping yard officer. He heads for the basketball court gathering energy while he walks. Using fire to purify the basketball court sending energy out to the four corners. The snow and ice burn away and walk towards the center of the court.

He sets the brush down and opens the paint.

He begins to chant.

Magic Paint Black as Ink

Make it Real What I Think

According to the Spoken Law

Make it Real What I Draw

Sigils start to form in a circle around him. As

the circle completes he starts to chant.

Ma'at mother of All

Hear my Call

Come according to the ancient pact

I need you to make contact

This better be good mortal.

I require an emissary with Fate.

You ask a lot of mortals.

I know.

What could so important to you that you would risk the wrath of Fate.

The life of my daughter.

Who bloodline do you claim?

None!

May I test you.

Absolutely.

She takes a small drop of blood from his finger.

This is interesting.

What?

Fate said that your line is dead but here you are.

What line is that?

The line of RA. You could be a pharaoh if the old were still in place. There is a response and she is willing to see you. An ankh shaped portal appears as they step in the realm of immortals.

Greeting Ma'at are they still trying to kill you.

Everyday.

Come mortal, sit at the table and join us. You pose a conundrum.

How so?

You are supposed to be dead and your children should not even have been born.

Why that?

Because no one was supposed to escape Ra spell he cast on his deathbed. Which was supposed to end the reign of the Pharaoh forever. So tell me how you survived.

I don't know. I am just a hedge wizard trying to survive.

At least you do not lie.

These are your family's books. All it would take is a snap of my fingers and you all vanish. So tell why I should save your daughter when she should have never been born?

I will do anything to save her.

I am glad you feel that way.

Because the only way to save you daughter is to become a God yourself. Because of your bloodline you do qualify. Every so often A God dies or retires and the Mantle comes back here to await Fate to decide to use them again. Only four Mantles have to be worn at all times. Fate, Death, Time, and Nature. The rest sit until the time they are needed to be bestowed to someone. There is a celestial event happening in 2 weeks time. The accords need to be signed by then and the Well Spring repaired for the Earth to benefit from the event. So I am going to bestow on you the Mantle of Magic. It has the power to save your daughter. It knows everything that has to be done and in what order. Just a piece of advice. When dealing with the fairy realm even with the accords there beings you can not control. The Erl King is one of these figures; only open combat will get a deal with him. He can only travel to this realm on Halloween. So you got time to figure out how to deal with him. Yes Time will help you. Here a fortune token. I do not give these out lightly. They can change even Fate itself.

Expect a pardon within the hour. The mantel knows the rest.

I can not walk around in this.

Only another God or Immortal can see it on you. As a prismatic Mantle is set over his shoulders. You no longer require an emissary to visit here but don't abuse it either. We All have our own Mantles to attend to.

Chapter 2

He reappears in the prison as if no time has elapsed. He returned the leftover paint and brush to his neighbor. Heading to his room to begin packing. He takes out a plastic case and begins to use the Mantle to enchant to store all his stuff.

While he waits for the call. 30 minutes and the call comes for him to report and he is informed to pack all his stuff and come back down. He leaves a note for his cellmate and grabs his case walking out.

Thank you and goto the Sergeant's office, he is expecting you.

I do not know how you did it but here your pardon and release papers. This one is your vital documents and cash out of your account. There out front with your bus ticket and car to take you to the bus station. I hope you make it to see her. That I will. At the bus station, Martin cashes in the bus ticket for the cash and for the bathroom. He taps into the Mantle and constructs a portal to the hospital.

He walks through to another rest room. He walks to the desk. Can you tell me what room my daughter is in? Name Cady Seelie.

She checks the computer. I am sorry sir but it says family only. Do you have I.D. Of course and hands over his license. You come along ways.

Yes I came right from the airport. She in 512 just take the elevator up to the fifth floor and should be to your right. He heads up. Stepping out of the elevator and nurse asked if he could be helped. Room 512 please, End of the hall on the right.

Her mom just left and didn't say anything about visitors. Can I see I.D. please.

He shows her his driver license. I am sorry sir we can't be too careful with kids.

It's ok I understand. Is it too late to order a tray?

Not at all. Are you staying a while till she leaves.

Yes sir. He heads down the hall and knocks on the door. You need to close your eyes before I can come in.

Ok. They are closed.

He opens the door and walks in. Ok you can open them now.

Daddy, Mommy did not say you were coming.

As soon as she told me you were here I made arrangements to come.

What are they telling you?

That I am dying and nothing can be done about it.

Let Daddy take a look at you. Martins taps into the Mantle. Talk to me . What am I looking at?

A nasty virus. It is eating her alive.

I was told you could fix her.

There are many spells that can save her, that is the easy part. The hard part is whether Fate will still let her live. Things fixed with magic can break in other ways and magic can only do so much.

Fate said that you could save her.

Hope for the best. Here is the best spell to accomplish this.

He watches the virus cells start to burn up. After he sees that everything is clean. He stops chanting and time resumes. How do you feel sweetheart.

Kinda fuzzy like I missed something.

You're going to be fine.

Wanna play games there a lot in the cabinet.

I hate to interrupt.

Mommy!

The nurse called. I was still close so I came back. So what miracle did you pull. He shows her the pardon. That still does not explain anything.

You would not believe the truth.

Try me.

I made a bargain with the Goddess Fate.

Lie to me some more. You lied throughout the whole relationship.

I told you that you wouldn't believe me. You'll see when the Doctor comes to check on her.

What did you do?

Saved her.

I don't believe you.

Just wait and see.

She walks outs.

A few minutes later she comes back with the Doctor and Nurse.

Young lady, how are you feeling.

I am perfect.

Can I run some blood work to make sure that is true?

Knock yourself out Doc. I am better now.

What makes you think that.

I just know.

Run a complete blood panel. So we can see if this girl is as healthy as she thinks,

Yes Doctor.

Mr. Seelie, may I talk to you in my office. What deal did you make and with who.

Does it matter?

There are very few people that make and let alone power a Mantle with power like yours. So yes it matters.

Ma'at and the life of my daughter. I take the Mantle and put some plan into effect. To help restore things in this world in 2 weeks. The celestial alignment. I guess I don't know.

You don't know what you're supposed to do and you agreed to do it to save your daughter. What Mantle do you carry?

Mercury's Mantle. I needed help in med school and that was the price.

You couldn't save my daughter.

I am assuming the rules of the Mantle were not told to you.

What rules I was told the Mantle will tell me what to do and what I needed to know.

They told you nothing.

Other than that, it was the only way to save her.

The Mantles can't change fate. The Mantle can fix minor things but major is just beyond are power. Such as a terminal virus because Death has already spoken. For Fate to intervene in anything requires an act of the council of Immortal to do anything. Just so you know your ageless is not immortal. What did they tell you?

I have a day with my daughter then I have to get started doing what the Mantle tells me to.

Let me give you a word of warning about the Mantles, they will try to control you if you let them.

Let's get back to your daughter and see how she is doing.

Daddy!

What the results, Doctor.

To be honest I have no scientific proof to support it but your daughter is 100% healthy. I am going to rerun the test in the morning. If there is nothing abnormal I see no reason to keep her. I have rounds to complete if you need anything else just ask. He leaves.

I still don't believe that you made a pact with God to save her. I have to get Caleb but I will be back in a few.

You both have fun.

Daddy there games in the closet.

Daddy did you really make a deal with God.

No Sweetheart. I made it with a Goddess.

What the difference.

Gods are male and Goddess are female.

Can I be a Goddess.

Maybe one day if you're good and stay healthy.

There was a knock at the door. Sir I am sorry to bother you but the Doctor asked me to bring this to you. He opens the box to note that says free will is important, wear this it will help. It is a coin on a chain. One side is the God Janus and the other side is Mercury's Caduceus. He slips it on and realizes all the voices in his head are quiet.

Daddy what is it?

Just a note from the Doctor not to wear you out.

Oh.

He takes out some stuff and magically makes a necklace for each of the kids. To allow him to communicate with them. Here honey I made something for you. Who the other one for. Caleb. Oh. He puts it on her. No matter where you are, you are able to talk to me.

Like a cellphone.

Something like that.

Aren't you staying.

When the sun comes up again I have to go. I will be in touch sweetheart. But I have to honor the deal that I made that made you better. Don't worry I will be in touch. Don't worry I will be close. Soon I have a big house and you can come stay with me.

Really?

Really Really.

Don't go making promises you do not intend to keep Mommy Says.

Caleb go meet your Father. He runs up and hugs him.

I got something for you. He shows him the necklace. Anytime you need me just squeeze and talk I will hear you.

So who is winning Caleb asks.

Cady.

Why do you want to take over?

No you in a bad spot Dad right now.

How is that?

In 2 moves she wins.

Why are you telling him that?

Cause you win too much.

Everyone laughs.

A knock sounds, sorry to interrupt but there is a pizza delivery man at the desk. I got this and walked out. He walks out and the orange aura around him. Hephaestus sends his regard and this. He says you need it for what is coming in the battle.

He takes it and the pizza.

Does everyone know where I am?

Just as you can, use the Mantle and find any one in the mortal realm, so can everyone else.

Why that?

It kind of Fates way of keeping track of active powers.

There is no way to hide.

There are always ways to hide, you're just not ready for any of that yet. Oh.

He walks in with cheese pizza for the rugrats and pepperoni for the adults.

How did you do that, you don't even have a phone.

I have everything I need to accomplish my goals.

How is that I already told you all of that.

Why lie?

Why do you think I am lying?

Because it can't be the truth.

Why not?

It is a myth!

Maybe not. He makes flames dance in his hand.

That's so cool the kids say.

This is not a trick is it.

I called in a favor with thee Fate to save Cady and this was the price of her doing it. In the morning I start working for her.

Doing what.

Making things happen that are meant to happen.

To what extent.

There is an event happening in 2 weeks , after that I don't know, for I can't see the future so I don't know.

So why make the bargain?

Cause I do anything to save her.

When do you leave to do all of this?

As soon as the sunshines tomorrow.

Have you told her you're leaving?

Yes I explained it to her.

What was her reaction?

She wanted to come with me.

If I know what to expect I might just have let her come.

I get it.

Now explain how you ordered pizza without a phone?

I can't because I did not.

It was sent with a messenger.

Good or Bad?

In different ways. I will deal with all of it come tomorrow. He moves his piece on the game board and Cady shouts I win!.

What do you kids want to do?

I am sure that we have a little time before the nurse comes in to put you to bed.

But.

But nothing. You were sick and need your rest.

If you want I can help you rest.

No Daddy, I am fine. I am going to take him home, and do not make me regret leaving you two alone.

Ok.

What on the tv that we can watch.

Knock Knock. Hey Doctor. You're not here for more blood.

No, I wanted to know if I could borrow your Dad for a little while.

Can I come?

No where we are you might make someone else sick.

Oh.

When we are done, I will bring a wheelchair and we can go to the gardens and see the flowers.

That sounds fun.

Ok.

Dad fix the kids please.

I'll try to help sweetheart.

They head out.

Where are we going?

The one place that needs a miracle to survive.

A few corridors later they end in a long hall of beds.

Who is that guy with the swirling vortex of doom surrounding him.

That Janus. He is the God of Chance. Mostly he oversees gambling, but once in a while he comes to hospital to help give people a fighting chance at life.

I thought they were fixed events.

Janus is a chaos emissary, he is not bound by the rules of Fate. He can actually extend the life of some of the people here and a few other tricks to help counter Fate.

So why am I here?

Only magic can help these kids.

Janus is here to ensure the ones you help do not die from other things.

What am I supposed to do?

Just let the Mantle guide you.

If you are the God of Medicine why can't you do all of this. I am bound by Fate you're not.

How is that?

Magic is a neutral system. It is neither bound by Fate or Chaos and can use both.

Ok let start with the most severe case and work to the easiest. Don't tell me anymore, I want the Mantle to tell me what I have to do and if I can do it or not. He looks at the first patient and sees a body covered in a black oily substance. Where are we, Doctor?

Oncology why?

I can't help this one. Janus is probably the only reason he is still alive.

You are kidding me. No, the foreign substance covers 90% of the body. To remove would kill him instantly.

There is nothing that can be done.

This one has one chance according to the Mantle.

What is that?

Mary Mallon's Butcher knife is said to remove disease.

What would it take to get it?

It hasn't been seen for a very long time.

So there is no hope.

There hope so long Janus can keep the cancer out of her brain.

Why that, can you find. It might take a day or two. The Mantle is hopeful that we can find it in one of the caches around their world. It must be somewhere.

Ok I see what Janus can do time wise.

Let's check the rest of your patients.

Why are all the kids here?

Because they do not make the choices that lead to cancer.

So they can still be helped.

This is the second most severe patient.

Don't be shy little one, I have a daughter you age. Maybe when we're done I will take you to see her.

Tell me you can help her.

I can but it's going to hurt and there will be marks you have to explain to the parents.

What do you need?

A basin. The Doctor goes to the cabinet and pulls out a basin returning with it.

I am sorry young lady this is going to hurt but you will be better afterward.

Promise she wheezies.

He grabs her by her rib cage and his hands sink in.

The girl screams out.

A minute later he pulls out the cancer and drops it in a basin.

I can breathe again, she says. Thank you she says as she hugs him.

This goes on for several hours stopping only to eat.

That leaves just him.

You are sure you can find a cure.

I will look tomorrow as I gather items to complete the capstone.

Keep in touch and let me know what you find. I will.

Oh I did try to clean up the marks as best I can but there are still residual traces.

I'll see what me and Janus can do about them.

He walks down the corridor back to his daughter's room.

Did you help them, she asks?

I did all that I could do for them.

Knock Knock. I made a promise to show someone the courtyard. I brought someone to meet you. This is Karen.

I am Cady. So you're coming to the Courtyard too. Yes.

Oh.

What are you here for?

I was here to die until that man made it so I could breathe again.

That my Dad.

He is a good man. I know he just makes a lot of mistakes trying to do the right thing. He always tries to do the right thing but somehow screws it up. Last time he was on time out for 7 years.

Wow, that is a long time. I am sorry.

It's ok he called all the time.

We are here girls.

This is beautiful, they say. How long can we stay out here they ask.

For a little while then you both need to rest.

Ok.

Daddy when are you coming back?

Hopefully soon honey.

Let's get you back in bed.

Are you going to be here when I wake up?

I don't know sweetheart.

Do you want to put you to sleep?

No thank you. But wake me before you leave.

I will sweetheart.

He opens the map and lays it on the table.

What am I looking at?

Looks like magical sites all around the world.

Avalon, Atlantis, Bermuda Triangle where

Calypso's Island is.

Who Calypso.

She fought against the Gods during the Titan

war when the Gods first came to be. There

Atlas's Chamber, The Well Spring, and a few

locations I am not sure of sir.

We will check them all out tomorrow.

Yes sir.

What do I need to do first?

First you need instruments.

We can probably raid the ancients caches for most of the stuff that we need but we will have to go to Eden to make a staff for you. You may want to get some sleep yourself, I will wake you when it is time to leave sir. It seems like only minutes as his brain clicks back on. Master it is time.

He rouses himself. Thank you.

Cady, yes Daddy. I have to leave now.

Are you sure that I can't come?

I am sorry I wish that you could.

You have the necklace if you need me.

Yes Daddy please be safe. I'll try.

Chapter 3

Where to Master?

Calypso's Island.

Why there?

Just something I remember about ancient Myths.

Yes Master.

They disappear and appear on a beach. As fireballs zoom over his head.

I am sick of heroes coming here and leaving.

I freeze the fireballs. I am no hero.

Then you can't be here.

I came to rescue you.

Why would a God rescue me?

They have left me here for thousands of years.

I know I read your story before.

I can hide you in a pocket dimension. It is under construction but you won't be stuck here anymore.

How long?

2 weeks a little longer. Once I have the ley-lines up and running I will be able to protect you better.

Protect me from who?

Fate.

Where Zeus.

Dead.

Your Lying.

Based on what I can tell only about 10% of the Gods of this world are still active.

What happened?

The Mantle says a renegade happened that wanted to rule the world and destroy everyone.

Fate took over and the Gods splintered. Now everyone is fighting for themselves.

Why help me when everyone has forgotten me.

No one has forgotten you. They have books about you now.

Then why does no one come anymore.

These days of heroes have passed. They are rarer now then even in your time. Technology rules the world.

Why save me.

Cause I was once imprisoned and it was not fun, plus cages suck.

What happens in two weeks. Magic flows through me. The Groves will be built at the nexus points.

What happens to me?

You will be able to travel again.

I am hoping that once magic returns I will be strong but Fate still calls the shots.

I might be back here.

That won't happen. I just came to get you again.

You think it will be that easy.

Zeus built this prison with the help of Poseidon.

The magic barrier was made by Hecate, I can't pass it.

I'll show you how.

He opens a portal. That your pocket dimension looks like a whole world. I am trying to make a place where magic and mortal creatures can live together and be protected. Not being hunted in extinction.

Why do you care so much?

Like I said I was in a cage and it was not fun.

If I agree what is in it for you.

I have an ally to help me.

Why me?

I just became a God yesterday. I do not trust the agenda of those that came before me and I am just trying to make it on my own. So I am trying to find one person that has my back and can hold their own against a bunch of power houses.

So you want to start a war.

No but I will defend myself if attacked.

So you're self righteous.

No, I am just trying to survive.

What your plan?

Make magic work then I don't know.

We're going to need a few things from the cave. I thought it was just crystal.

That what the stories say anyway.

No it where I make things to fight Gods. You're kidding me. Every hero gets something to succeed on their quest. So let's find you something to complete your quest. As they walk in she touches a few crystals and a wall opens to reveal; several looms, a forge, and somethings he can't identify.

How long have you been making things.

Since I received a message that a male would come free me and need this stuff.

You're joking now.

Nope it happened over 2000 years ago.

That was impressive.

She is the reason I let heroes come to visit me.

What is all this anyway?

I made weapons, armor, and other items to disrupt a Mantle's power. See this globe it absorbs electricity. Cool. Do you have something we can pack all this stuff into?

He pulls out his case and they start packing things up. This should fit everything. Once it was all packed.

She comes out with a sword.

What that?

Something special. You need this on your belt. No one will see it but me and you.

What it does it do?

Trust me you will need it but I can't explain what it does.

Ok, as he ties it in place. Do you want to go into the pocket dimension?

Yes anywhere is better than here.

I'll visit nightly.

Go to this place next.

What is there?

You'll find your familiar in that place.

Oh and what is it?

Something from the old world that has been lost and you must restore it. She steps through the portal.

Do we have the power to make it? I am not fooling anyone but no one comes here anymore. Chanting starts and a double of Calypso appears. Master you know your job. Yes sir. Mantle why do we need to hide her. Because without the Well Spring I will die in 2 weeks. Let's check out this mountain hideaway she suggested. You need to be careful they could be controlled by other Mantles. A portal opens.

Chapter 4

They appear in a clearing by a cave blocked by a massive orange boulder. Mantle why is the boulder orange.

It is protected by a Mantle.

What now?

We can attempt to pass through but whoever Mantle is connected to it will know if it is active.

Do we know who?

No Master the identity is unknown.

We will pass through and see what happens and hope for the best.

Master here the spell, He begins to chant and becomes transparent. Walking through the boulder. Inside is a great cavern. At the center is a slumbering silver dragon. Is that her idea of a familiar?

He is too old to bond with. There must be something else in here Master.

Just walk and see what we can find.

Too bad I can't take the horde. I will never be poor again.

Alchemy Master can make you all the gold that you will ever need.

That part of my domain.

Yes Master.

Ok then we will work on that later.

What is all this stuff?

Different Magical Items.

What the writing on the wall says.

ONE WILL COME FROM THE GRAVE TO SAVE THE WORLD FROM A LEGION OF FATES

Any clue what it means.

Prophecy can mean anything.

Ok After searching the cavern Martin finds a door. The door is unlocked. He opens the door and steps through.

Just to inform you Master, we have entered a pocket dimension.

Who does it belong to?

Technically you Master.

How?

It read that it belongs to the God of Magic.

How did you not know it then.

Some Mantles are told to forget and you do that. Yes, Master it is complicated. Sometimes we learn things that the world just can not handle.

I see that. Tell me what I am looking at.

It looks like temporal storage for Dragon Eggs. You can bond with one of them and it will give you magic without the Mantle or the Well Spring.

Do I pick one at random or is there a specific one for me.

Pick one from what I can tell.

He reaches across the eggs and one leaps into his hand. Do I need to do anything?

Just hold it till it hatches.

Cracks begin to show and a metallic rainbow colored dragon pops out and dives into his chest.

What happened?

 It bonds with your soul.

Can I merge this pocket dimension with the one I am already creating.

Yes Master but it would give Calypso access to the eggs.

She can pick one if she wants.

Is that wise Master.

It would make her more powerful than she already is.

Yes here the spell then. He chants and the world shifts. This is coming along nicely. I tried to make it based on the climates in the records.

It is wonderful.

Where is she?

Under the tree.

I think you call it napping.

He calls out for Calypso.

Look what I found.

What is it?

Come look.

She gets up and heads his way, That's going to

make a big breakfast.

There are dragon eggs.

You can take one to see if it will bond with you.

My kind is not meant to bond with creatures.

But if you think it will help. She walks around

them. Is there something supposed to happen?

I had one leap into my hand.

Like I said not meant to bond.

It's ok.

What else are you going to do?

I might send a dragon in here if I can wake.

Oh God a living dragon.

Don't you think that a bit much.

It might be but he needs a new home like you
do.

I think I might have exposed him to Fate.

Did you see this?

No. What is this a crystal ball? For what.
Usually messaged play when you hold it and
see if it plays.

My name is Merlin. I leave this message for the
future. If you found this it means the alignment

is near. These are things to aid you on the quest. But the Capstone must be fixed before the Alignment happens. I built the Capstone to help better regulate magic in the world. Someone destroyed the Capstone hoping to get control of the magic. But all that happened was the Well Spring closed itself to magical overload. I was unable to find the immortal responsible for the collapse of Capstone. I imagine that they will try again. Good luck and hopefully you will take care of the dragons for they are the last of their kind. They will hatch when binding with the soul of someone they connect with regardless of magical aptitude.

The Glass cracks into dust. That was not helpful.

Go get the dragon and I will try to take care of
it.

He appears back in the cave. He chants and
the dragon and horde slip into the pocket
dimension.

Why didn't that go he asks as he walks over to
it?

It is a staff.

Should we take it?

You still have to make you own.

We will have to deal with that I guess.

He walks towards the entrance and changes to
pass through the boulder. He was greeted by
men with guns.

You will surrender any and all artifacts from the
cave.

Says who?

The Coalition Force.

Piss off comes from his mouth as a dragon leaps from his chest off the head of the lead guy.

Holy crap he has a dragon.

Lightning streaks the sky and the bullets that Mantle are absorbed. When the smoke clears all that is left is charred remains.

Boss we are in trouble.

Why?

Mortals know about dragons. They were dead how long and these people acted like they were normal.

Good point we will add it to the to-do list.

Take use to Eden I can make my staff. Even with your help that was draining.

There are other instruments that we can make that can help in that regard. As the dragon matures you will be able to draw on his power. The portal opens and they walk through. Come on Swirl. He hops back into his chest.

Chapter 5

They appear between angels with flaming swords.

What brings you here immortal the voice booms.

I am here for the materials to a staff.

You may pass but don't eat any fruit.

Yes mighty angel.

He walks through the gate between the walls.

What is an angel?

An outsider, a creature from another plane that was brought here. You see a lot of things here from other planes.

Can I populate my space with them?

I wouldn't.

There are no predators or prey in Eden. They don't have to hunt to survive. They are given everything. You don't have the power to do that.

Oh.

A fireball whizzes past his head. I prepared a defense Master.

I thought there were no predators in Eden.

Magic doesn't come from animals.

What are we looking at?

Probably an outsider or demon.

I recommend we hide until we find out.

He chants and vanishes while walking down the path.

They come to an ambush spot. 4 demons are detected under an invisibility spell.

We know you have one enemy sir. These belong to Hel.

That a place not a person.

She is an underworld Goddess that rules a pocket dimension full of demons and the offspring they create.

No one knows where they came from and they just appeared one day.

How do you destroy them?

You banish them back to Hel's realm but I never seen one destroyed.

You said all animals exist here.

Yes Master.

We need a cocktrice.

Why?

I am going to try and see if I can petrify them.

That is a bold plan but how do you plan on finding one Eden is endless.

How is that?

It was big of a world and a stone in the sea.

Quit with the metaphors.

It is a world of its own.

That was created to be perfect.

That is why mortals aren't allowed here.

Can we just call a cocktrice to us?

We can try.

There is a spell that allows communication with animals.

He draws glyphs on the ground and chants,
Ancient cocktrice come to my aid. I need you to
turn these demons to stone with your magic
gaze. They wait. Should we try again?

If it does work a first time it wont work a second
time. Even magic fails once in a while. As they
talk a giant chicken comes running out of the
trees.

I think we might have success. The chicken
runs through the ambush site and all that
remains is stone statues.

I walk up. Is this effect permanent?

Unless someone has mandrake extract.

We can leave them here can we.

The angels will see to them. We lost enough
time.

There the tree. Pick a fruit and bless it in the pond at midnight.

When that?

About 8 minutes give or take.

Just tell me when. As here pulls a ripe apple from the tree.

You can proceed at any time now.

As he dips the apple in the pond and a female appears.

I am Isis.

You are a long way from the Nile.

I go where the moons shine.

You must be the dead man that Ma'at found.

That is I.

So you come from the most ancient and magical wood in all the universe to make a staff.

Tell what makes you special.

I am not special at all. I just made a deal to save my daughter. This is one of those steps to complete this goal.

What if I refuse my blessing. Fate has enough power without adding magic to it. You're new for more direct challenge.

I have been told if you refuse your blessing I am to just to seek out the sacred oak.

That second rate wood won't help. Fine you can have my blessing, as she touches the fruit.

I will give you a piece of advice. If you plan to challenge Fate search out the 4 eyes. 2 are in Egypt, 1 is in Norway, and the last is lost in time. If you want others to only speak the truth look for Aphrodite's Golden Apples they grow in a pocket dimension on Mount Olympus. Farewell and good luck Ra for your power will be restored.

What now?

Place the fruit on the altar and hopefully receive the wood that we need.

Then everything is up to me.

He places the fruit. The fruit seems to grow into a 6 foot tall mini tree and it is a good thickness too.

Now what?

Let me handle the rest.

The tree begins a slow steady change. Here is the staff of Ultimate Knowledge. Just reach out and claim it.

Martin grabs it as a sensation happens. What just happened?

You know the complete knowledge of the world. Anything that is written you know now. That alot to comprehend. That is why mortals are allowed here.

I can see why.

Your companion is probably lonely and you need rest. The Mantle opens a portal.

Chapter 6

He appears in front of a stone house. She was busy. He walks in asking Calypso if she is here.

In the back.

He walks back to see her tinkering with things.

I see you're busy.

Not to complain or anything but did you have to make eternal daylight.

No it changes with a thought.

Where have you been? You smell strange.

I just came from Eden.

Dealt with demons using a cocktrice.

Open the case where we stored everything.

Next time use this, it turns demons to dust and traps their essense for later spell work. That handy to know.

Can I ask you a question. Are you planning on marrying me or am I free to do what I want.

Honestly your life is up to you. Once I get the Groves up I let you out of the pocket dimension.

What happens after that is completely up to you.

In that case you're sleeping in the other room.

That's fine with me. Are you ok?

Just worried that someone is going to notice that I am missing and come look for me.

Let me show the Island and pulls out a flat crystal.

That me. How can that be?

I took a hair from you and made a copy.

Unless someone physically shows up on the Island they will never know your missing.

You did think of everything

What can you tell about the Eyes of the World? There are 4 of them given out to different pantheons to help monitor mortals.

The first is the Eye of Fate. You know this from Greek and Norse culture. When combined with the hair of a mortal it shows their whole life thread including the possible knots.

The next one is the Eye of Ra. It is said to be able to detect and neutralize pockets of chaos in the world.

The third is the Eye of Horus. It is a lesser copy of the Eye of Ra.

The last is the Eye of Odin. It is said to allow the user to look into all past events of a specific person or place and enhance a person's personality. If you're good you're really good and if you're bad, you get it.

Why?

Isis told me to them before I continued my quest. What that look for.

I do not trust Gods especially with these items. They are uber powerful and made for people at the time of creation. Do you even know where to find them?

Absolutely.

Then why haven't the Gods claimed them.

Most do not exist anymore like I told you.

I assume they can't claim the items.

But someone did move an item of powerful magic today shortly after my talk with Isis.

Be prepared and if you need help ask for it. I am always here.

Here is an amulet if you need me it can reach me anywhere. I am going to get some sleep. Goodnight.

Master it time to rise. He does and sets a lovely sunrise. Where to first?

Wait, you can't leave yet. I made something to help focus the power of the Eyes. She hands him a necklace.

He opens a portal and enters a museum in Germany.

The case over there Master. Your body temperature is evaluated.

I know what is missing and I am now extremely worried that someone plans to kill me before the Capstone is finished,

What missing cause it not in the records.

The Spear of Destiny.

I am unfamiliar with that weapon.

Do you remember a demigod around 0 A.D.

There were so many.

He spawned the Christian Religion.

You mean Jesus.

The spear pierced his side, and in doing so pierced his Mantle.

There are many weapons that can pierce a Mantle.

I am sure we can find one in the ancients caches. What now sir?

Cairo pyramids. Portal opens. I have Eyes to collect. They appear in the Burial Chamber.

That way sir. They run into a dead end.

What now?

Phase through the wall.

He phases through the wall into a tunnel on the other end. He walks through the wall and down a hall. As the ancient Gods of Egypt appear. Ra speaks.

There just a spell sir.

I am a descendant of Ra and have come to claim my birthright. Only those that pass the test may claim the Eyes. As beams shot from the wall. What is happening?

They are trying to penetrate the Mantle.

He opens the case and pulls out a disco ball looking thing. The beams shoot back to the place they originate from. I am Thoth the Guardian of Knowledge, I thought most of the Gods were lost and only still exist.

So why hide?

Someone has been killing off Gods slowly over the years.

Why here?

The Magic of Eyes masks the Mantle.

I can hide you in a pocket dimension.

That won't work.

It just has to work for 2 weeks.

Just leave the girl alone.

I can do that.

He opens a portal and watches Thoth disappear.

He walks to the pedestal. And there sits 2 glass Eyes. He places each one in the necklace as his mind opens to things around the world. I need a place to talk to Time without Fate listening.

You can send a request to his place.

In the Sands of Time make it happen. A minute later an hourglass appears. I see you claimed 2 of the Eyes.

I have.

I take it you want my help to claim Fate's Eye.

I have refused all offered to claim the Eye.

Why grant yours?

I don't know if you should or you shouldn't.

I am just trying what everyone expects me to do so I can make things happen.

The other wants you to make a stand against Fate.

Where do you stand with Time?

Fate is for mortals and it is irrelevant to Time.

By midnight you are on Avalon and defeat the Sleeping Guardian. It is in the center of the island is the altar of time. The Eye will appear for five seconds. If the Eye is not removed it will slip back into the time stream and be lost again. Remember nothing is free and he finds himself in the museum.

Where Northern Europe I don't see anywhere else to go.

They come to a well at the center of the museum. I see you have your eye on the well. Most people ignore it.

Cause no one remembers the legend.

Do you?

Odin pulled out his eye and cast into the well in exchange for a sip of the water.

So you're the one the world has been babbling about.

I have been around for thousands of years.

But can't be, I can't sense a Mantle.

I predate even them.

I am the Keeper of the Well. I know what you came for. But before you take it, please take a sip of the Well so you can see all the plots afoot. He puts the dipper in the water and allows me to drink. Suddenly everything starts to appear for me. So now you see how everything works. That is a head rush. Now you summon the Eye to you. I offer one last thing for you to consider. Find the last of the Golden Apples. Only the Mantle of Love can plant the last apple to grow a new tree. But if you can find one no one can ever lie to you again. The Eye appears in his hand and he attaches it to the necklace and another head rush.

Are you alright sir?

Yes, just a lot of knowledge to absorb. Can we shift to another plane?

So long as it is not barred from travel.

Where to?

Asgard.

Sir it nothing but ruins.

There is something that the Well says to get there.

Really.

Yes.

Enlighten me.

Just take us there.

Chapter 7

Martin takes Calypso's demon killing staff out. The next minute he is pulled into Asgard and is surrounded by demons. No sooner then he touches one then it turns to dust and the rod gems light up. The demons soon scatter. That way and he flashed in that direction. He climbs a set of stairs. The Flame of Eternal Life. He starts to chant. A small phoenix appears out of the flames.

Greeting Master. So finally someone has come to claim me. Place your hand in the fire and see if you're worthy. He places his hand in the fire as if it wasn't even there. As the back of his hand burns and the fire is extinguished. The emblem of a phoenix is tattooed to the back of his hand.

Sir you may be able to heal that boy now. The phoenix has wonderful healing properties. Take us to the hospital and let's see.

At the hospital.

It's good to see you Mercury. Say you have a cure for the boy.

Something with potential.

He was over there with Janus.

Young man, I am not going to lie, this will probably hurt alot.

I don't care. Phoenix rises and cleanses the boy. Fire engulfs him and winks out in second.

I can't believe you found a phoenix.

They have been lost forever.

I think this is the last one.

Treasure it and it will treat you well.

I plan on it. So it worked.

Janus more than worked. Let's pull his life string a little more. 40 the best I can do without breaking him.

Well it was better than he had.

Where are you sending him?

Don't know yet. Where are his parents? There are none.

When he wakes, call me. I might have a use
for him.

I don't have an issue with that .

Janus?

He has no prospect in this realm.

Ok just call me.

Sir was going to need a boat to travel to
Avalon.

Why can't we just portal there.

It is a blocked realm.

Even going by boat we could be blocked but it
is highly doubtful.

There is a marina not far from here.

As they leave the hospital bullets begin to fly.

Bullets can't hurt us.

Enough of anything can be deadly.

Let's get out of here.

Shadow walking is the best. As he steps into a shadow.

Welcome to the shadow realm Sir. Head that way. It will let us out by the water. They step on to a pier.

Let's see about a boat. They head for the Dock Master. I need to rent a boat.

Credit card.

Here you go.

Dock 3 Craft y-30.

Thank you. They board the boat. Once there on the water.

Here the spell, As they leave he chants and mist swirls around them and an island appears.

Three women appear.

We are the Ladies of Fey. Why have you come?

I have come to reclaim a magic item and renew the accords with the Queens.

Leave the craft and walk to the island.

The Queens will meet at the Starlight Pavilion. Touch nothing but the item you seek. Don't disturb the sleeping King for it is not his time.

He steps out of the boat and strolls across the water to the beach.

Angle that way for the pavilion. They arrived at the Starlight Pavilion. There he sees two ladies drinking tea.

Come join us. There is a cup for you.

Thank you Ladies.

So you come for the Eye.

Among other things.

I brought a new Accord for you to sign.

So the mortal world is finally ready for its return.

Magic is a risk and I can't open the Well Spring without having the Accords signed by you both.

I know Let's see them.

He pulls them out. Dragon skin.

I thought they were dead.

They are alive and protected.

Oh then you will want to visit the Dragon Knight in the cave over yonder.

He might help.

There are your Accords signed.

The Eye is at the center and don't get distracted.

As they walk across the island.

There stopped by a lady standing on a lake.

I can give you a sword of great power. No one will stand against you. The greatest king to wield this sword and he was king of a nation.

No thank you. I believe in making my own power.

She fades back into water.

You did good for her.

The cost outweighs the benefits.

You would have replaced the sleeping king in his sleep.

Really.

Yes it is how it works.

Yes it is how the king has lived for a thousand years.

Oh

Come we only have about 10 minutes.

Why so short it barely midday, when we came here.

Time passes differently here.

That much.

You could be here a year and day would pass outside.

I guess we need to get this done and get out of here so we do not miss the event.

The event happens here at the same point it happens there.

But you just said the time is different.

Look at the sky. See the alignment. Regardless the alignment happens once in a thousand years for Earth but here thousand years could pass.

There is the altar.

He grabs at the weird glass as it hits the altar.

A glass cat's eye appears in his hand.

Interesting.

What sir?

Just the shape.

I was expecting something different.

Shape depends on who holds it. For Merlin it was a glass globe. Some other shapes include a mirror, crystal ball, and even a silver plate. The most unique is a dagger.

Can we portal out of here or are we going by boat.

Boat sir.

Can I fly or is flying restricted to?

You can fly. But shouldn't we meet the knight.

Mind as well but I don't want to lose more time.

We won't.

I will watch.

He set to the sky.

Over there is the cave based on what the Queens said.

They land in front of the cave. Hello anyone home. The Mantle radiates light as the darkness is seen all consuming. They eventually reach a lit central chamber. A dragon lays curled in the center.

Welcome magic man.

Why does he sleep?

It is an enchantment because the Fey do not require food, so there is no prey for this one.

So he just sleeps. Why not return to the world?

No thank you. He is the last. I am not about to watch him be dissected by what you call it.

A doctor.

No not a medicine man.

A scientist.

Yes that is what I see in what the world has become and want no part of metal birds and self driving chariots.

You said the last, What if I said that he was not the last.

Then I say you were mistaken. Swirls come out.

I know we're napping but how they were all killed by Merlin. I have currently; one unbound dragon and 149 eggs. I want to start a school and train people to care and fly dragons.

You know once you are bonded to a dragon you can't die unless the dragon dies.

I figured something out. But I only have a limited knowledge base which is why you have come to see me.

I didn't come to see you. It was just a happy accident that I was visiting the Queens and they told me about you.

Oh.

So no one but Fey even knows I still exist.

Sorry. It is not your fault.

I came to protect him and can you tell me how long I've been gone?

Merlin has been gone a thousand years.

He goes to the mirror. Show where you are going to build your school. Just tell it and it can show anything in the world.

Show me the Colorado Rockies.

That much land can narrow it down.

Not without surveying and seeing what towns are nearby. I want a place that only magic can reach.

Smart plan. See that glade. Build it there.

Why?

Surrounded by mountains and I don't see a path through the mountain to reach it.

I check it out and let you know. Do you want to come with me? I am sure you can be useful when I build my school and me and you will teach.

For now I think it best to be hidden. Break this, it will let me know you're ready. Godspeed young one.

I hope you realize your dreams.

As he zooms out of the cave. He sees his boat just floating there. Why the boat here, it should be farther south.

Avalon is a living creature all on its own.

You make it sound alive.

It is in a sense. Just like the Earth is alive or more so. Avalon is actually conscious. The Earth Sleeps. You will see when you leave. They board the boat. Don't cast, just sail and we will arrive where Avalon thinks we need to be. As the fog clears.

Chapter 8

They see StoneHenge appear. Where the Well Spring.

The place where all magic is said to come from.

We have to complete the checklist. I thought.

Avalon has a different plan or is trying to tell you something.

What the status of this? 93% complete and a pile of magical debris covering the Well Spring.

Is there anyway to cloak the site from magical sight.

It already cloaked.

He covers his eyes with silverlight. See the strands, there a kind of protection covering it.

Then how do we break it.

It will take a lot of scanning.

Let go see Heapatus and get something to syphon the debris and see if he still has the apples He cast a teleport spell and it fizzles in his hand. How far do we have to go make it magic work.

Not sure.

I guess we are walking until then.

Sir an opening in the net but it seems to be guarded by a furry thing with fangs.

That looks like a bigfoot mated with a vampire.

Do we anything in Calypso's bag of tricks.

It catalog but we have no idea what most of it does. Your best bet is to use your staff or the staff from a the dragon's den they should work.

He pulls the staff and chants. A blast of energy exits the staff and hits the creature.

I am sorry puny God you can't leave. The mistress says if you leave, then I must die. So fight me.

Do we have the power to make me match his size and muscle tone.

I can increase your size and muscle but it is only for a short period of time.

Do it. He doubles in size and muscle mass., Charging the creature.

He recovers quickly and is resistant to being pushed back. Sir we need to cross the barrier if you hope to win. Martin grabs his arm and attempted to throw him throw him through the barrier. He flies but not far enough. I charge for the opening and just feel the flow of magic as my ankle is seized. The creature crosses the barrier pulling me off my feet.

Mystical Call I summon lightning. The creature hairs stands on ends and he drops Martin. Who quickly escapes using a portal.

I see you met one of the several creatures lost in this world to stop you.

It seems immortal.

Nothing is immortal just like everything it has one or two ways to kill it. What you met was a wendigo. Highly dangerous and hard to beat. Silver is a good way, suffocation is another. If you can get it in the water, drowning is the most efficient way because it sinks like a stone. So what do you want first?

The apple. The apple comes with a price.

What is it? There are only two left. The first has to be planted by the Ageless of Love. You will find that person. The problem is true love is rare nowadays and therefore finding someone to represent it is near impossible. Do you accept the challenge?

I do.

Then you may have the last apple.

The Mantle must be placed before the event.

Magic and Love go hand in hand.

Got it. He eats the apple.

What is wrong?

Nothing just expecting a head rush that did not happen that seems to happen everytime magic works.

With this you only have a rush if someone lies to you. Then you'll know the truth of the matter.

Now a syphon. What does the debris look like?

He shows him a picture. Interesting. By the looks of it the well should have absorbed it.

What do you mean?

It like any well all the garbage sinks to the bottom of the well to be broken down. This stuff just floating on top blocking anything from coming out. This should do the trick. One word of advice. FInish the Capstone first before activating it before you use the syphon. Thank you. Can I ask a question?

Sure.

Where the forge?

That so last millenia, now everything is factories and mass production. Invention is tricky nowadays and people barely experiment like they used to. Sorry, it 's ok. I find someone now that is worthy of making something. Good luck and if you find someone attractive to be my wife.

Come again.

Love and Creation are destined to be together that is why I choose the Mantle holder. One last thing plant in the middle of Nebraska and wonderful things will happen. Ok Before or after the event. Doesn't matter when you plant it. It will happen once the debris is removed.

They head out and find themselves in Japan. I was not expecting that.

Watch out there are things here older than the Mantles.

Should we seek them out.

I doubt that we're here if it happens.

We will deal with it.

I figured you know why he sent us here.

He picked someone for the Mantle and wants us to place it because he can't do it. That lady by the Cherry Blossom is my guess of his choice.

Can I talk to her?

Sir you speak and here every language.

Good. Greeting young lady. Do you believe in true love?

I think that it once existed but people no longer believe.

Would you restore it to the world if could.

I am only a peasant farmer that life would not be for me.

If you will come with me I can see if it is your life.

How just follow me and I will show you, He opens a portal and they show up in the Hall of the Gods. Take that Golden Heart.

She does and is engulfed in a pink light.

Take this apple and plant it somewhere special. Take this portal, it will take you to a man that will help you.

Thank you.

Chapter 9

Come out Fate I know you are there.

You had no right to give up that Mantle.

Actually I had every right.

It is not time for love to walk the world.

It is always time.

You know you sentenced her to death.

Because it is the only way to return a Mantle here.

I know the evils you committed trying to control the world. You killed Gods and stole Mantles for yourself. You either draw the spear and attack me or go back to your schemes.

The spear appears as she charges straight into the portal.

What did you do?

Choose a more appropriate battleground.

You can try but you can't do it.

You can't stop me leaving.

Try if you like but we're sealed in. Even if you beat me you'll still be stuck on this Island. Come fight me and explain why killed or arranged to have killed so many Gods.

Cause I can only absorb a Mantle being worn.

How many have you killed?

Hundreds.

Why am I telling you this?

You are ensnared by the love apples.

No one can lie around me.

Are you going to attack me or am I just going to pull my trump card.

She charges with the spear.

He dodges and slams an elbow in her back.

How can you dodge my attack without me foreseeing it.

That your problems you think you see everything. I was running around for a week thinking I was your obedient little puppy.

But you have gone everywhere I thought you went.

And a few places you never dreamed of. Come and I'll show you,

See what you can do.

She strikes at several spots.

He slams a palm of his hand in her face and encases it in a living flame.

It burns.

The flames burn out.

How you get past my Mantle.

Something even you couldn't predict.

It can't be it dead,

Nothing truly dies. For rebirth is always

possible with the right elements.

You can't do that. It is forbidden.

Nothing is off limits to me.

You think that.

I know it. I am the best of two worlds.

She charges mid-sentence.

Checkmate and jams his sword into the center

of her Mantle.

That's your trump card.

Just watch.

What is happening to me?

The Mantle is breaking into the original parts and choosing new hosts from around the world.

Why Fate most always exists.

I am going to leave on this prison island because unlike you I don't believe in murder.

There is a cabin up the path to your new home.

Have a nice time as he phases out.

Chapter 10

He steps into the council chambers as new people start arriving and older people start to sit.

So Master of Magic you started a new council.

Now what.

How you figure all this out?

Someone left me a map of clues and a prophecy.

How she did not see the prophecy.

He points towards Apollo's Mantle, cause he wrote the prophecy and walked off the job so she couldn't learn it.

That explains a lot.

So many Fates are there now?

9 of them plus 23 Mantles of prophecy.

That's a lot of power.

How did she hide it?

With chaos.

That is impossible.

She can't touch it.

He tosses the beads on the table.

She was wearing these the whole time. I have been around it enough and they radiate chaos.

But why?

To control the world.

The more Mantles in play the more control Fate has over everything.

I am the oldest on the council and you are telling me Fate had control because there wasn't enough Goods to say otherwise.

Yes Fate is only part of the equation. In most pantheons a council has always been led or headed up by the supreme male in that pantheon. Now most of the pantheons are thanks to Merlin who devised a way to merge Mantles of the properties that could rule the domain instead of clashing with one another. That is why instead of thousands of Mantles there are only a few hundred.

Can we merge all the Fates back together. Yes but that would be counterproductive,

Why that, Janus asks.

Cause one Fate can't oversee the whole world. There are too many things that are being left undone or uncared for.

Like what asked Time?

When was the last time anyone has even looked at the Tapestry of Life?

Based on what I can make out of it, the world ends in 4 days.

How can that be?

The event is still a week away,

That's it.

That something the old Fate failed to tell you.

She was the only one to see the event.

How is that Death asks?

Because she was going to absorb all of you into her Mantle as the world ended.

I am not certain about you Death you should have to harvest all the souls of the departed so you might have been exempt.

What people like me that don't live in the mortal realm. Your pocket dimension would collapse as the mortal realm vanished.

Now we need to vote on who is going to lead the council and I am not taking the position. I have enough to do.

Arguing ensues.

When a pip squeak of a girl shouts for quiet. This is exactly why the old Fate did what she was doing. Cause you are all divided. Even though he does not want it, the Master of Magic set this in motion and has to lead us.

Cheers.

Do you have a little girl's name?

I am Harmony, third of the Norns.

I thank you for the vote but I do not want it .

You have no choice, it is your destiny.

How can it be destiny?

You see the writing on the wall, as much as things happen for a reason.

There is a great threat coming and unless you lead us then we will lose.

I have schools to open and magic to unleash.

We all have lives beside the Mantle.

Your 9 what do you have to do?

I am 10 thank you. I have a family. Why most of you are grown and can walk away from your life, I still have a bedtime and if I am not home for it. This Mantle can't save from the wrath my parents will bring against me.

There was something you were told and have not even thought of it.

What you are a descendant of a dead line.

Do you ever realize what that means for the world as a whole.

What is that?

Apotheosis can return as long as someone from Ra line lives to challenge him.

It was Ra who cast that spell on his deathbed.

Even now both Ra and Horus's Mantle are missing.

I am still not seeing why it has to be me.

Look at this way. You are now the only Pharoah left. If it is not you then who else.

The oldest.

No thank you. I have a hospital to run, that is enough.

Fine I agree then what do i do.

Just what will I doing.

Explore, build, and let the world know that we exist. Find this one God this world has come to worship, live and bring him before the council.

I'm sure between you and your Mantle something productive can happen.

Fine I will lead but don't expect any slacking because your ten.

Here the Hammer of the Council. It has the ability to summon one or all of us to this chamber. You can let the cage bird go. Those who want her life have long since been absorbed or dead.

Ok thank you. As soon as the Grove is planted I will. Is there more business to discuss? I have a lot of work to do and only a week to do it. Also I am finding that there is a Supreme being head hunting me. Anything else.

Athproso raises her. As the oldest of the Fates.

How old are you?

16 sir.

You are the oldest.

Not in age but my Mantle lived the longest.

Ok that a better explanation.

There are things that keep happening that shouldn't be happening. Timeline. The last 2 decades maybe a little longer.

You are telling me this, why.

Cause when I put the tapestry back in order these happening will change.

The mortal won't even notice but the Mantles will.

What the most important event. Chernobyl is probably the most significant.

It was not supposed to melt down.

Not at all sir.

Set something up for all the Mantles to know and be prepared.

Yes sir.

Can someone tell me why all 9 aspects of Fate are kids.

I am not a kid sir.

Who are you?

Melody Simmons. I am 21 and hold Clotho's Mantle. It is the youngest of all the Mantles. But the future belongs to the young so it is up to us to set Fate.

That at least makes sense.

 Anything else.

Yes sir I am Mandalynn and I am the Oracle of Delphi. I have a prophecy and a question.

IN THE 8TH MOON THE SNAKES WILL RISE TO EAT THE SUN

When can you restore Apollo?

When I see someone worthy unless the Fates want to clue me in on who to choose.

The tapestry is a mess. So I doubt it, if I untangle the right thread I let you know.

I may have some insight into the dilemma.

Who are you and what is that? I am Sky, the middle of the Norns.

What are you laughing about?

Your name and your hair. I can't help it.

What do you mean?

If it changes color based on my mood.

Is that the Mantle?

Nope been that way since I was born.

Then I may have a present for you.

Really I like presents.

Reach in the bag and pull it out.

She does. It is an egg.

Just give it a second.

The egg hatches and prismatic dragon appears, Meet Prism. Once I open the Dragon Academy you will have to come to train.

Shiva chimes in there, supposed to be extinct.

I got 4 living dragons and 148 eggs to disprove that.

I doubt the hair was tipped off. Anyone who can change their hair or eye color can claim a prismatic dragon.

What about the other dragons?

So far all the eggs that have hatched have been prismatic in nature.

But I was told I know if there is someone who can claim another kind.

Who told you that? The great Merlin who collected all the eggs around the world.

Oh Can we try.

I don't have an issue with that.

They line up one by one.

They reach into the bag and come out empty handed.

Satisfied.

For now but if you find more please make the council aware.

Of course.

Now Sky you had an idea about Apollo.

There is an award winning harpist touring Europe right now.

Apollo has always been about a harp.

Seems like a good choice.

But you do realize that the last Apollo a guitar and had no fame what so ever.

Just try it that all you can do.

I am off to Nebraska to plant my Grove.

Wait!

What is it Sky?

I can't take a dragon with me.

Just tell him to come and see what happens.

Come boy.

He dives at her chest and disappears.

Where he go?

Look at your chest.

So now I have a tattoo, Dad is going to love that.

Once I get the Academy running you can let him run loose all you want.

Thanks, an Amulet appeared.

If an emergency happens call me. He disappears. It is in the middle of nowhere but there is a node beneath the soil. Perfect. He calls someone. It covers all areas in hundred miles in all directions. He plants the tree and mighty oak sprouts and buildings start to appear. He pulls Calypso and everything out of the pocket dimension. Welcome to the Grove, I can't believe it.

You are free to do what you want. You can go anywhere you want.

Anywhere I want.

There is one restriction, you can not go visit your father.

Can I ask why?

He has definitely not learned his lesson and even to this plot the fall of the Gods.

You get into trouble just call. I am amulet away.

Ok.

I've been told that you'll be left alone but to be safe do you want any gadgets or gizmo back.

No you'll need them before long.

No not every God is on your side even now. Ok safe travel and watches as she fades out.

It's just the two of us now. StoneHenge needs repairs why the syphon takes care of itself we need to find the stock piles. Ok so take us to StoneHenge.

Chapter 11

Calypso sits at the center of the ring.

I thought you were exploring.

I almost got hit by some metal beast with a family in its belly.

It was called a car.

What is that?

Think of it as a self driving chariot.

Oh. That is interesting, I should have invented that.

It's ok at least I have help.

What are we doing?

Picking these two stones up and then going to the mountain. To make a top stone. Then we are going to align them to the moon, If it works

we are going to get a pretty light show.

Ok I am in. But you're going to show me how

this thing works.

Hold still I can do better than that.

What are you going to do?

Just He touches her forehead and everything

that his brain holds is transferred to her.

That was reckless but fun.

You were a mean person before you went to

prison.

Very and I never debated about that.

Why?

Because I was scared of life and love.

I kept everyone at a distance.

To avoid being hurt and then I got hurt.

Then everyone left.

At least your kids love you.

Yep and now I am free but too busy with everything else to be there for them.

You can always see if a dragon will pick them or give them the magic spark to come to the Grove.

I can't worry till this thing that is supposed to show up after the alignment is beaten. Come on my Magic Man I will help you get the stones up then we can have a picnic lunch before heading to the mountain.

Sounds good.

As the place the 2 stones a rhythm starts in the air.

I hope that is a good sign.

She pulls a cloth out of thin air and sets it on the ground.

So what are we eating?

Whatever the cornucopia produces.

A banquet appears.

So this is how you eat on the Island.

No, the Island produces enough for one person to live, but a hero left it for me. He said, "I was not eating enough." They have a wonderful lunch.

What are you doing?

There is enough wildlife in the area to eat the leftovers.

Soon all the food is gone.

They head towards the mountain.

Hold on to me.

Why

I am going to flash us there. Ok.

There is a cave.

There is nothing there Magic Man.

Just trust me.

He pulls her into the cave.

Sir we left the mortal realm.

Where are we?

The land of the Dwarves on the outer planes.

It explains why the materials do not register to earthlings.

Can you map this?

Yes Sir.

Then do it.

Ready for a little exploring my dear Calypso.

Absolutely.

They wander for a while and come to a chamber with a crystal ball in the center. Martin walked up and touched it.

Welcome Master of Magic. This chamber is sealed. This is where I mined the stone to make the Capstone. In the event that I didn't finish those who plotted against me have succeeded. There is only one chance to finish the Capstone. In the back of this cavern is an out of place gemstone. In there you will find a cache of weapons hidden by me and there are others scattered around. I secretly and planned on Arthur having them if he awakened. The weapons go to him. For he will know how to set the world straight. If he still slumbers, only one bound by time can awaken him. Use the cache to get things right for the coming. For he is immortal and destined to rule the world.

The crystal ball dissingrates. He walks to the back wall. Looking at all the gems. I don't even know the name of them all.

Now what asks Calypso.

Crystals are your thing, can you figure that out.

He waves her over.

Can you tell what stone doesn't belong?

There is a lot here and more types than the mortal realm.

Just look it over and let me know.

She stares at it and finally declares that like a yellow flower is the only unique one.

You sure.

I had my own crystal cave of course I am sure.

He pushes the flower and the floor starts dropping to reveal a staircase.

The stairs wind down to a chamber with a dragon sleeping in the center. Interesting guarding Merlin's stash.

Are you going to send with the other one.

The thought crossed my mind.

I think it is for the best.

He opens a portal under the dragon and it goes though.

Let's split up and look around. He finds staff, wands, and magical items. He hears a yeep and flashes over there. What are you ok?

It jumped into my hand.

I guess you meant to bond with a dragon after all.

As the egg hatches a yellow snout pops out of the shell. He cute.

Her he corrects.

You can tell.

I can talk to her and once the bonding complete so will you.

It ok Topaz you just scared her.

She zooms up her and perches on her shoulder.

What do I do now?

When I open the Academy we will find out together.

For now just make her feel comfortable and bond.

He begins to bag the eggs.

What the total she asks.

348 unhatched and 5 living dragons. I am guessing that the last piece you needed.

What is the writing?

It says do not teleport it, carry it out with levitation.

I guess I will try and he casts a spell and it floats.

They start to climb the stairs and it follows.

As they leave the cave there is an assault by large insectoids. Calypso draws a sword from nowhere. She starts to dance and slices through things like paper.

Fire alights as Martin chants.

Soon after nothing but exoskeletons litter the ground.

That was intense.

What were those things? Chaos Bugs.

Not really sure they have a name. He taps the Eye of Ra and sees the portal that let the creatures in.

Can we close it.

Ra's Eye should have the power. A web appears over the portal as it shrinks into nothingness.

You did good magic man.

Let's get this rock in place.

Chapter 12

They place the rock and beams of light shoots everywhere. As the light fades Martin can see the camera crews.

Are you an alien?

No my name is Martin Seelie. In 6 days an astrological event is going to take place. With the event comes the return of magic to this world. The first training center is the center of Nebraska. Tomorrow I will set one in California, Louisiana, Virginia, and a small island north of Chicago. As the weeks progress I plan for 3 in Europe, 4 in Asia, 2 in Africa, 2 in South America, and 1 in Australia. I have time for a few questions. People please make them relevant and short.

Who will this calling go to?

It is completely, by chance. you can't buy, or pray for it. It just happens.

What if someone knocks over Stonehenge again.

I will be monitoring very closely. One more question then I have business to attend to.

Does God exist?

There are many Gods and Goddesses in the world right now and more will be coming. I have to meet the Christian, Jewish, or Arabic God that their bible said made everything. Thank you I will have another press conference the night of the event right here.

Him and Calypso disappear in the mist.

What business do we have.

I am taking you to a concert. As he waves his hand there clothing changes.

You do not have tickets.

Of course I do.

I have a whole box just for the 2 of us.

My word you work fast.

Aww Mister Seelie your box waits and he will meet you at the conclusion of the performance.

They sit. What are we doing here.

Trying to see if he the next Apollo.

You have doubts about him.

A Lot of them. He just a stuffy.

From what i read Apollo has been creative and free.

Not always

What do mean.

When Apollo's Mantle started it was about it sun and worship.

Eventually he found how things were and they flowed from there.

I hate to give him bad news but his twin is dead and absorb by Isis since there Moon Goddess.

Can I ask you a question?

Of course Calypso.

Do you believe in soulmates.

It be stupid after everything I have seen.

Could you be mine.

Anything possible.

There is a way to know.

I can ask Fate of the Goddess of Love.

Can we after the shows over. Sure.

As the show concludes someone comes to show them to the backstage area. Mr. Seelie I am very busy so lets make this quick.

Take this harp and we will talk so long as you are not a pile of ass.

He takes the harp and nothing happens and I don't see a Mantle.

How is that possible?

No clue sir.

Sorry to bother but it is ancient and I wanted your opinion.

Of course Mr. Seelie.

How old is this?

If you believe my family it is 3000 years old.

Nothing about the wood is right for a harp.

I am not an expert on wood but I would find someone who is.

I will find someone.

Thank you have a pleasant day.

We need to go to Ma'at temple in Egypt.

There is something happening in Asgard. All that was there was Hel's demons.

Shift us there. They appear to see a man fighting with a sword and losing ground quickly.

They pull staves and quickly go to work on the demons.

Thank you strangers. I thought I was just free to be killed by those things. I am Heimdall watcher of the worlds and guardian of the Bi-Frost.

Not anymore Asgard is Hel's terrority.

She can't be here.

There are rules.

Odin and Thor are both lost right now.

You are the last serving Asgardian.

There are 2 others in the council chamber. I was sent to light the ancient fire and wait for help.

I am the only one coming and all I can do is take you to Midgard.

We can't abandon Asgard good sir. The elves, dwarves, valkyries, and fallen heroes will come.

I don't know about the elves but everyone else belongs to Hel at this point.

There are either dead or Hel's slaves.

How long have we been trapped in the council chamber.

I do not know. I had come the other day and freed a phoenix and here we are. You have the Eye you can look into the time stream and see.

He told the Eye to look. 2000 years since Odin sat on the throne and kept Hel confined.

This is not good. The girls are not going to like this at all.

Grab my hand and they wink to the council chamber.

Where the army.

This is it, your majesty.

You lit the fire and only he came.

He says everyone is either imprisoned or slayed.

Lovely, now what.

I take you to the immortal council on Midgard.

What will we do?

Oversee mortal events. Live a life. There are endless possibilities.

Any chance of rebuilding Asgard.

There might be if we fight Hel.

But I got too much to do right now to start a fight right now.

But how can you kill an immortal?

You are not immortal, just ageless. No one is immortal, not even her.

Thor's power sits in a cave waiting for a mortal to pick it up and become a thunder God.

So all hope is lost.

No just on hold. It is on the to do list.

Ok I guess we will go with you.

Do you know what freed us?

I can only assume that it is claiming the phoenix from the Eternal Fire.

You didn't. I did.

Why? It is what kept Asgard thriving without its life force the planet will die.

Chapter 13

He opens a portal and they step through. He takes the hammer and slams the gong. Everyone starts to appear.

It past my bedtime what so important.

I want to introduce to some old Gods I found on Asgard.

Asgard is dead Ma'at states.

I know that, they were trapped in building and recently freed. They don't have a place so I thought you all make them feel at home.

Ma'at if you can stay the rest of you can go.

Come with us a couple Gods drag off the Asgardians.

Is this real.

You can't tell.

I thought it was and even presented it to a candidate. Nothing happened.

Only by breaking it can I test it.

Break it then what happens.

It if legit the Mantle finds a new host. and if it a fake it just becomes wood chips then.

She snaps the harp in half and nothing happens but it a decoy.

It got to be somewhere.

Yep just like the thunder God.

When are you being him back.

When I find someone worthy of a Mantle.

Let me know if you find a Apollo's Mantle.

Could it been absorbed by another Mantle.

Anything is possible.

Artemis was taken over by Isis.

You realize that.

Yes.

Just like I know you have the titan Gaia in you.

Not so as have but it is extension of myself.

Gaia is primordial. If she wanted she could easily shred Ma'at and assume control.

Oh.

But if she had control she would release things only seen in nightmares.

Oh great.

Exactly.

Why doesn't she.

Nuclear holocast would kill her and she not ready for that. Oh. She was absorbed along with the Green Mother, to try and keep things balanced. I must go I plants to attend to.

I believe Sky is waiting to talk to you.

Thank you.

I see red hair this can't be good.

You are meeting my Dad.

Dad why?

Cause someone explaining a 14 year old has dragon tattoo on her, and why her room is destroyed and colored rainbow.

He laughs.

It not funny.

It is a little bit. Come I'll fix your room and put everything back the way it was before it broke.

Thank you.

They poof to her room which is destroyed.

I saw battle fields with less damage and she did it all.

Yep.

Ok.

He waves his hand and the room is as good as new with the expectation of a small crystal statue.

Why didn't you fix that.

Its resistance to my magic and the only thing I met that was resistant to magic is a Mantle carrier.

I like to keep it until I can solve the mystery of it. I want it back.

It's important.

To you or the Norns.

I'm silly.

Let's dip into the time stream and watch the breaking and see what it tells us. He touches the Eye of Odin. Interesting a pink Mantle. They shoot back to the present.

Ancient Wall
Hear my call
According to Spoken Law
I Summon Time

Yes oh wise Leader of the council.

I need advice.

At least you ask before running off.

What would happen if you took me back in time to stop a Mantle for being released.

I can't affect a Mantle worn or in an object.

So I am just stuck.

No I can tell you where it went and when it left.

It in South America, and it is Aztec and named Queacotzl.

So can I see her.

That is up to you.

She never been part of council and I doubt she will join now.

The best thing you can do is join her and Ma'at and hope for the best.

Thank you.

Can you fix it a non-magical way?

Yes I do have super glue.

What the deal.

It the last thing my mother gave me before she died.

I am sorry, call me in the morning and I'll meet your Dad and explain things. Hands the statue back to her with a small seam. Here it in this and it will be safe.

Thank you.

Maybe after all this I will introduce you to my kids.

Do they have dragons.

Not yet they will.

Oh see you in the morning kid. He fades and appears in the Grove.

I am glad your here for bed.

Sorry problems.

Did you help Sky.

You know. Red hair was a dead give away.

I told her I meet her in the to try and talk to her

father.

Oh you didn't sleep with her.

Why would I.

Your male.

I am not that kind of person.

Well take me to bed and you can have a

reward. In the morning.

He waves his hand and clothes food appear.

Where are you off to?

To see if I can fix Sky's issue.

If you can't.

There you going to have a companion here,

cause I am not going to leave her defenseless.

Ok then.

Do you want me to come or I can meet you at Stonehenge.

When I am done I will meet you at Stonehenge.

Chapter 14

He phases into the world and pops out just north of London. He knocks on the door.

What the little wanker has done now.

Sir I am Mister Seelie.

The man from the tele.

Yes What can I do for you.

I like to talk to you about Sky.

What she done now.

I can pay you.

I am sorry but I am not here for that.

Then what do you want,

I am here to recruit her to a special school.

She useless.

I am sorry but I can't stand you anymore!

Sleep! Sky come down here.

You killed him.

No but he won't wake for a few.

This should fit everything.

But.

Do you really want to stay with a drunk, that thinks you are useless.

I guess not.

Go pack and I will leave a note.

She comes back real quick.

What you pack.

Just clothes and my crystal statue.

Ok. Let's go.

Do you want to come with me or go to the Grove.

What at the Grove.

Just empty buildings.

I will come with you.

He opens a portal. Stepping through. They do not appear at Stonehenge.

Where are we?

I do not know just yet.

Sometimes magic takes you where you need to go, not where you want to go.

Prism you mind as well come and play, there is land a plenty.

Hover Lights. Analyze surrounding. There is nothing in the memory. Anything magical on the scan. There is a magical creature just south of us. Maybe it will help us get home.

This way Sky. Stay close. Swirl comes out and keeps Prism company.

What is that?

The guardian of the land.

Greeting Ancient One. The lead is dead now. I am the land. Soon your world will look like this. This is the Quartz Realm home of the Crystal Beast. But I am all that is left. Do you wish to leave this world?

Where would I go?

I have a pocket dimension where you can go.

Alas without my statue I can not travel.

Where is it?

Destroyed like everything else.

I have a statue you can live in, Sky says. She pulls out the glass statue and he is instantly attracted to it.

That will work as the crystal darkens and the beast disappears.

I guess the threat they talked about is real. I guess we can go now.

This place is strange, she says.

Sure as he tries to open a portal that won't open.

I guess we are not done yet.

Call your friend and see if he can aid us.

What can I do for my new friend?

Why can't leave.

There is an altar to the north.

Maybe that will yield you the answers you seek.

Climb on I will carry you. They climb on and the

dragon flies off to the north.

Do you have a name she asks?

I am Clement of the Azure Sky.

I am Sky and this stick in the mud is Martin.

He does not look like wood.

It is an expression.

They fly for 30 minutes.

It is the only statue that survived.

The creatures are lost.

Are you sure?

I have flown the whole globe,

I am sure.

What do make of it?

Something connected to the Gods of this land.

Ancient Statue Black as Ink
Summon the Person that I Think
According the Spoken Law

Bring Forth the Person that I Call

I am the Leviathan who has awakened me.

I am Martin Seelie and someone called me into this land and now I am stuck.

So you are the destined savor of the Crystal Race.

I am the last. I will grant you my power to you.

A new tattoo appears on Martin's forearm and the statue shrinks into the palm of his hand.

Use this power wisely and bring my people to a new home.

Now I think we can leave.

You know your going to kill yourself if keep collecting powers like that.

What should I do to let him die?

No but there has to be a better way.

I research it. He opens a portal.

Chapter 15

They go through the portal and appear in Stonehenge. You both smell like ash, you did burn down the house Calypso asks.

No we just visit a dead world, and the thing that killed it is head this way.

The syphon is working.

How come no one is talking to us Sky asks.

We are shielded from sight, I did one interview that is enough.

How can I help you Athropos?

I have been fixing the Tapestry but nothing goes past 2 days after the event. He due the day after the event and if we don't win nothing else will matter or we can't do anything about it.

Ok

Just so you know.

What next the girls asks?

Planting a Grove about a 100 miles from here. He spent the next day planting Groves and putting portals in place people can use. As the tree grows he spots a cave opening, The three enter the cave. About a mile into the cave everything changes.

This stuff looks Native American, and boring Sky says.

The walk way drops into an open cavern. There is a crystal in the middle and the message plays.

Greeting Immortal. Welcome to the end of the world. These crystals hold the knowledge of all the world. At the time of the alignment the Guardians will awake and almost be in place for doom shall on us like a rock. The crystal turns to dust leaving a prism in its place.

He picks up the prism and holds it in his Mantle. The wall opens to another grown dragon and a bunch of eggs. He portals the dragon to the pocket dimension.

Sir a spot appeared.

For what?

I think a dragon egg sir.

Flash us all there.

They appear to a red-haired teenager. Who are you he asks?

I am Martin Seelie and I here to offer you a once in lifetime opportunity.

He takes out an egg and said take this the little guy wants to meet you badly.

He takes it and the egg hatches.

That Sparks and he your new best friend.

I am homeless and can't support myself led alone thing.

Just follow me and you will be take care of.

He opens a portal. This is the beginning of the Grove. DInner at the other end. You two have fun.

Why test them they already been chosen, Calypso asks. One is a Goddess.

Cause magic is part Chaos and anything can happen. Ok. Twenty minutes laters Sky appears.

Was that necessary. I did not need my Dad drunk wanting to beat me. It is a lesson in controlling over overcoming fears and not letting them control you. You passes so what the problem. I saw things. I didn't want to admitted even happen. Do you want to talk about it. Do you know what happen. I know everything that even been written down. Then no. You knowing is enough for me, Just know I am here if you change your mind.

Where the boy Sky asked?

Zach and Sparks should be showing up any minute.

Don't tease him to badly for wetting himself.

What the hell, how could you know that. I know everything.

Would you like me to clean you up.

I guess.

With a wave of his hand her clean again.

The rooms are all empty. Boys to the right and girls to the left. I will know if you cross the Grove, so just don't .

But.

You are 14 just because of who you are doesn't mean I treating you any differently than I would the other.

Goodnight we have 4 days and there going to be busy.

He leaves with Calypso. Tell me how the egg thing happen.

It just informed me.

Just informed you. I wish they all do that.

3 Caches on the map that we can reach.

How many can't we reach. One owned by primordial God from before the Mantles and the other only a Sea God can reach.

What that?

Atlantis.

Can we flash there.

We could but we would die. It to far down.

Ok so we get the 3 Caches and go talk to this other God about the last Cache then. Sounds like a plan, good night. Soon they drift off to sleep.

Chapter 16

Now probably the best time to talk to God and bring the Titan he might respond better. He leave a magical note for Sky and Zach. Come Calypso we travel. He opens a portal and steps on a volcano know and Mount Sinai. Ancient one I summon you and one that speaks of the past. The sky darkens and the thunder booms as a blue dragon descends from the clouds.

Greeting Godling and daughter of Gaia. What can I do to help you.

I seek entrance into the cavern in the volcano.

At least you asked.

Your past Master asked me to guard it till the time was right.

What makes you think that the time is right.

The event is in 3 days and he who was expelled is coming back.

Interesting. How do you know this.

Prophecy spoken by an Oracle.

No one has told me this but my domain does not extend past Japan. Go with my blessing and try not to disturb the mountain to much.

He flies off.

Let fly. They dive for the cave entrance.They walk through and head down into the volcano.

How far?

I do not know.

We just walk until we get there. After a while they come to a door. He chants and the door opens. They see a dragon. He is huge the biggest they even seen yet. He opens the gate and the dragon slides down. Now we just look around to see what he hid here. Ok. That start to look around and rock monsters attack them. She pulls a hammer and he wields a mace. He chants and chips fly off. This is not working, he tells her.

Try fire or acid. He backs up and starts throwing fireballs as the thing explodes in pieces everywhere.

A key lays on the floor. Grab he tells her. I think I saw where it went. Begins to examine a section of the wall. Right there.

She inserts the key and twisted it with an audible click.

The rock slides aways from the wall revealing a massive chamber full of a thousand eggs, clothing and armor. After hours of collecting everything and then they find a harp. I that what I think that is. Break and find out. She snaps it and blue light flies out. Let lock up and get out of here. They portal to the next cache.

Chapter 17

They are met by a group of Ninja. Your head will roll down this mountain. They draw swords and attack. Sword fight ensues, Everyone is bleeding as the Ninja retreat into the smoke. They should not have magic.

It is not magic, just a cheap trick. There in the trees waiting to follow us. Let go to the entrance the magic way and give them something to be amazed about. As they both disappear from view. They approach an orange opening. This stuff again,

You saw it before.

Once at the first cache I raided.

There is a boulder covered in it.

It smells like orange blossoms.

Oh, hold my hand as we walk through it. He chants and passes through the wall.

I was expecting more out of this. I don't know maybe an explosion.

Let everyone know where we are.

This place looks empty like someone has already raided it. Guessing by the skeleton it was a while ago.

How they pass the barrier.

There are more immortals to count than there are stars. Any of the ageless could, maybe a dragon master, or a fey could slip in, and that is not counting all the outsiders running around.

I get it to many magical bad guys running around.

Let's look around just to be sure.

A minute later Calypso calls out and gets something.

Can you read it? I can try.

He who finds this. Know that my this, that the gifts were taken to protect the world from misuse. The bones might still have some use if you know someone who can forge them. Signed Merlin

Than why no crystal ball.

Merlin did not write that.

How can you know that.

No magical signature.

Impressive.

We can take the bones to Hephaestus and have him deal with them.

What weapons did we lose she asks.

I can look into the time stream and see who has them but I am not expecting much. They are probably masked and mortal.

You think so.

Yes.

He touches the Eye of Odin and time races backward 522 years to a group of masked ninja emptying the place.

Well I do and do not who did it.

Who?

They all wore masks and looked like the guys outside.

Who are plotting to jump us as soon as we leave.

Wonderful.

Dragonbones into the case.

They exit and as the group moves towards them he yells time stop. Everything but him and Calypso freeze. He unmasks and photographs them all. He starts time and they all fall. No momentum. I know who you all are I just want the items back.

Smoke appears and they disappear.

Now the last 2 cache to get to. They portal to

Scotland to an underground building.

Just behind a door.

I am being called,

ok I wait here.

I am Athena, where Zues.

Lost, dead, no one really knows. Right now I

rule. I am sorry you been locked away for so

long but I need to talk to Mantle holder.

Hello sir. Wear this it will help you stay in

control. Do you have a name?

Beverly.

Where you from?

California.

Do you want another Goddess from Cali to

help you out.

Sure cause I am definitely confused.

Mandalynn I summon you and bangs the gong.

You know I have school.

Yes and I will write you note if need be but she need your help.

Athena or Beverly.

Just Bev.

Ok. I'll you understand all of this.

You what 16.

Yes I am close to that.

What were you doing to be claimed.

Running an Owl Sanctuary.

That explains why she picked you.

So her where you to can talk.

She waves her hand and picture pops.

You 2 behave. I'll see you soon and he portals backs to Scotland. I open the door.

It just another pocket dimension full of eggs.

He collects the eggs.

Let check on Sky and Zach.

They pop in to find them kissing in the courtyard.

No one being forced.

No then ok.

Wanna break for lunch or should we leave you 2 alone.

Lunch is good.

If you're going to do stuff just.

Not a virgin.

Have the knowledge of Fate.

I think I am good.

A table full of food appears and they eat.

What have you been doing?

Check the Well Spring, collected more eggs, met Athena and I thought it was going to be Apollo.

So sorry.

It's ok.

But everyone wants Apollo, but no one has seen him since Merlin was around.

What is the plan after this?

I got a stockpile in the middle of Mongolia.

It is going to be very cold and dangerous.

So I assume you want to come.

Of course.

Without people this place is boring.

I was my hand and we are all decked out in ski gear.

Chapter 18

The portal opens and everyone walks through.
Swirl come out the land clear of people, Topaz,
Prism, and Sparky joined in.

What are we looking for?

I thought of a cave but I am not really sure.

Just let your Mantle look for something out of
place.

Look around and see what you can find out.

So icy wasteland.

Do you think we're standing on it?

Let see if I can clean the snow. What can I
see? Fire purify. The fire fades to reveal a
small opening covered in the red ward domain.

Sky we found it.

You cheated we were digging in the snow and
you just melted it.

You recognize this.

Yep War but he is sleeping somewhere.

I am thinking of him right here.

He phases them through. He gives them all glow bulbs and tells them to call out if you see anything. About a half hour in the search Sky says she found something. He comes over and reads the inscription.

I CAME TO WHAT I THOUGHT WAS THE END OF THE WORLD TO STOP THE FIGHTING. ALL I FOUND WAS MORE FIGHTING AND REALIZED THIS MANTLE TO DIE FOR THE WORLD TO LIVE, SO BURIED IT HERE. I HOPE THAT WHOEVER FINDS THE SWORD LEAVES IT HERE. SO ENDS THE LORD OF WAR

This stuff is ancient. I am not sure if any of this will even work. Then we will bag it separately.

Even if I know it will still work.

He pulls the sword from the wreckage of bones on the floor. Magic sheathing it.

Sky tells me does the myth between War and Love come into play or can I pick anyone.

Anyone should do it.

Put this on Zach and draw the sword. He soon engulfed in a crimson fire. I am the Lord of War.

Good just what I want.

I know you are kissing on Sky but you might fall for the Goddess of Love.

Why Fate sucks sometimes.

I can tell you she is a cute Japanese girl.

You do realize you rewrote his whole Fate.

Good or Bad.

If you don't win in 3 days it won't matter.

Let's check the syphon and then I will take us all to dinner.

Fun where.

I don't know any place.

None of that created meat. Dinner is on hold and my kids need me. He portal them to Louisiana to a trailer.

Chapter 19

What wrong kids?

Mom sleeps there and boulders in the kitchen.

Big mean guys calling for surrender.

I 'll handle this.

He steps outside and freezes the boulder in the

air and sends it back.

A ring of giants appears.

Send me your leader.

He can cross the fire unharmed,

Battle me one on one.

For you have errored attacking my family.

I am Golith of the Nephilim.

We wanted your attention and had no quell with you. We seek your power to send us back to our parents' world. We are half outside and have been here since the one God called Lucifer Morningstar from his world and sent him to Earth. Then he refused to send us back where we belong.

Tell me where I can find this God and I 'll send you back.

A temple somewhere using the name Buddha or Gnosh.

Here is your portal.

Now leave!

50 of them file in a single file into Eden and 2 angels.

The angels won't like that.

They are there off-spring and let them deal with them.

He comforts his kids and uses his magic to fix the trailer.

Reach your hand in the bag and grab one.

They each select an egg.

Caleb gets a baby blue dragon named Sapphire.

Cady gets a prismatic dragon named Rainbow.

They will help protect you if anything else happens.

Mercury I summon you.

Yes.

You said your power works on minor things.

Can you revive her?

Simple , she woke up.

That beam hit me.

Just a nightmare.

I brought presents for the kids.

There baby dragons.

You didn't.

I did.

Show her.

They hold up baby dragons.

I will collect them for dragon training school next week.

Mercury poofs out.

You're not taking them anywhere.

They barely know you.

But they need to learn all about dragons.

As they get older they will need more care.

I will think about you, your girlfriend, and whoever kids there are going to be around.

Come kids, hugs, then mommy wants me to leave.

Ok.

Be safe with the dragons.

He opens a portal to the Grove alone.

A little sneak appears with her dragon.

So you can't stay put.

I wanted to come.

Mom is going crazy about you leaving.

But I have an hour before I have to leave.

Where are you going?

To see if I can find an Elven Army.

Why?

The end of the world is coming.

When?

The event tomorrow night.

Then Apophis is supposed to rise.

I have to fight him or the world dies.

I am going to open a portal and send you home.

I will worry enough without you being there.

I wouldn't be able to fight.

Ok I go home but you better come get us when this is over.

He opens a portal and she sinks into it. Calling Rainbow. We have to go. They both vanish.

Come folks we are going to Buddapest. They portal to India. We are looking for the biggest Buddist temple.

That way by the looks of it.

So someone finally came looking for me.

He has a lot of Mantles, Sir and that means power.

I am God.

You are made up of many Gods.

I can tell by looking at you this predates Merlin's Device to unite Mantles.

So your story definitely interests me.

First I need to know why you're hiding?

The end is coming.

Not good enough.

It is peaceful here.

What is going to happen?

Please. Story.

The heads of the Pantheon got together and one foresaw the end of everything . So they sacrificed themselves and power to create me. I am the culmination of everything. Then I met a man named Buddha and Shiva. The Gods in the area.

She ignored me. I'm staying here.

I need your warrior side to come out now.

There is a war coming.

I was destined to survive it and make Utopia.

Boring.

He swings at him.

This is unusual, I can't see your actions.

He rams his sword into the center of the Mantle.

Lights begin to fly off in all directions.

What have you done my collection is leaving me.

There are all gone.

You can go back to peace as an orange light strikes Martin in the chest.

A Mantle has absorbed sir. You now have the powerful Sun God Mantle of Ra.

You may live in peace all you want but I need the old Gods for what is coming.

Chapter 20

They all leave for the council chamber of the Immortal.

So how many Ma'at.

59 new mantles have appeared.

Zeus and Odin.

He looks on the military man by the look of clean cut appearance.

What the situation?

Undoing all the mistakes everyone made in the past has cost me time. The event happens in 12 hours. I still have to deal with elves for an army and bargain with Hel over the dwarves.

I can deal it can't be that bad.

She rules 3 other outer worlds right now.

Asgard been destroyed with only 3 survivors.

Is it really that bad.

I saw another world destroyed with only 2 survivors.

Have you seen my spear, my horse, or my ravens.

All gone. The only survivors are Heimdall, Freya, and Frigg.

They will be around once I summon the council.

Wear these, they will help you. He bangs the gong.

The age ageless start portaling in. Heimdall, Freya, and Frigg approach.

Do I know you.

You have the power of Odin but not his memory.

I am Frigg technically I am the Mantle's wife.

So you were not kidding that Asgardian could really be killed.

I am assuming that Hel has captured the other Mantles or there lost on Asgard.

There is a possibility that it is there and we do not know about it.

Zeus and Odin need help with the new world.

Just show them around. I have a Thunder God to find.

Would you like help from the Fates to choose a candidate or several.

That fine I will take them to the cave and have the hammer test them.

Does it have to be a boy the First Norn Sunshine asks?

No why?

There a science student that an unhealthy like for lightning. I will check her out.

Anyone else? Sky chimes there a guy in Canada named Thunder claims to have been struck by lightning.

Good I 'll check them both out..

He poofs out.

Him and Calypso appear in a Canadain woodland to see a beefy man cutting wood.

Getting flush he ask,

who are you.

I am Martin and you have the opportunity of a lifetime.

You and a young woman get to see who is going to be my New Thunder God.

Who is she?

I do not know yet I have not met here. Ok Ian.

They portal to an open courtyard and get doused in napalm.

Thank God for Shielding.

Someone threw chemicals at us.

For what.

Don't know what to do.

Swirl tackle them.

The guy is pinned.

So it's true that magic is coming back.

Scientific stuff and magic do not work together.

Not true, there is a thing called a technomancer that blands science and magic.

Can I be one?

Attacking the God of Magic is not a good way to start. I am sorry.

I am Charles.

In 8 hours you will know.

Why then because a lot of people will get the call.

Just answer.

Thank you.

Why are you here?

A Casey Elliot.

I will show you her lab.

They walk in to see tesla coils surrounding a lone cage in the middle of the room.

Casey, can I talk to you. Sure.

What is up?

I like to take you to a Cave and test you to be a new God of Thunder.

What do I get?

You get to wield thunder and lightning.

Sounds like a plan.

How are we traveling?

Portal,

So magic.

Yep.

Ok let go then.

He opens a portal as they all step through.

Ian you first, with pleasure.

He tries and strains but not even budge it an inch.

Your turn Casey.

I can't lift that.

You can if you're worthy.

It will let you.

She wraps both hands around the handle and lifts it like a feather. She is engulfed in a yellow and white Mantle wearing gauntlets and a belt.

Wearing this will help.

Let's meet everyone.

They get back to the council chamber to a war council led by Zach and Bev.

I brought another power house.

Thor good we could use another heavy hitter.

We could really use a Sea God for this battle.

I 'll see what I can do but I doubt it.

We got 20 hours before he appeared.

I got to see the event.

Go I got things here.

Him and Calypso shift to Alfheim. I came to see Lord Frey.

You may hold the Eye.

Greetings mighty immortal.

What can I do for you?

You can bring your elves to Earth to help fight Aphosis.

He arrives in 20 earth hours and I need you to fight with me.

What kind of area do you plan on fighting in?

The Desert and try to have home field advantage.

I say no.

Then I bring Odin here and compel you to help.

Odin is dead.

I revived him in my body.

You do not have the ability.

I do and show him the Phoenix mark.

Asgard is going to finally die just to save him.

Actually it saved several people including a little boy.

Defeat me in single combat and you may borrow my elves for your war. Thank you. As the challenger you get to choose the weapons.

Swords.

He talked to an elf. I hope you're familiar with a leaf blade. I have been known to dance with the wind, Frey comments.

Your choice.

Anything about them he asks the Mantle.

Just super deadly.

He picks one and they square off.

The battle lasts 5 minutes when his leaf blade breaks. They were enchanted.

They were not enchanted.

I would have known.

They're supposed to be enchanted not to break.

All the leaf blades are enchanted and this happens.

Someone deliberately disenchanted these, It couldn't have happened by accident.

I guess it's a tie.

So what do you need?

I need sorcerers, archers, and medics that you can spare. The fate of all the free world rests on this.

I saw him destroy one world and god knows who else didn't call for help.

After about 18 hours.

Sir there is a call from Sky.

She needs you in Nebraska, now.

Fare thee well Lord Frey. I 'll see you in 6 hours to start collecting your people.

Chapter 21

He portals into Nebraska. What up?

I tried to divide them according but I can't get them to leave their children and other family behind.

They just sit there waiting for you. Welcome people.

Those who wish to go to Magic School must pass through the Grove alone and unaccompanied. They have what it takes to learn magic. I will send anyone home that does not wish to try and the spark will die. Most won't even remember.

As a kid charges a tree, and starts to climb.

He disappears. He went to the Grove for his bravery.

I want my son.

Then you must go through the Grove.

He belongs to me now.

She runs to the Grove as do others.

Soon the magic sorts the worthy from the not.

He teleports into the Grove.

To see Zach Lord of War directing people to various cabins.

You guys have it here.

I am going to check the other Groves and he poofs around the globe appointing people to take charge of the Grove and directing people to the cabins.

Let them know that school starts in 2 days.

He teleports back to Nebraska.

A woman claiming to have lost her son.

He scans all the Groves for the lost boy.

Coming up empty.

Ma'am.

Katrina.

I am going to scan your mind for an image of your son, so I can find him.

Do whatever you need to do,

Just find him.

He quickly finds a picture of him and the boy in the tree.

He starts scanning for life signs in the trees. He locates him sitting on a branch.

He whispers to the poor boy.

Why make your mom cry.

She is my stepmom.

My parents are dead because I want to come here in the first place.

If you do not want to stay with her there was plenty of room in the boys dorm.

Ok I will hold you to that.

He hops down and shimmers as he walks.

Katrina I came here to get away from you.

You're not my mom, you should stop acting like it.

I am sorry I don't want to hurt you but I need myspace. I am a teenager now. There is plenty of space for me in the boys dorm. I plan on living there and being a man on my own.

Ok

fine may the God of Magic can end my life too.

Here your knife.

One appears out of thin air.

I know where you're going.

Where?

The Armory.

It is in a different grove.

You can still see each other if you want.

But I think this is the best move for you both.

Ok.

Step with me.

They disappear and he heads for the dorms.

Welcome to Chicago.

This is Hephaestus. He makes everything and will teach you how to make magic weapons and items. Any history. She pulled this out of thin air and showed him to Kris. Interesting an assassin's blade out of thin air.

Where do you get the design?

A book cover.

Oh so she can be molded.

Good keep me updated.

I got a battle to prepare for.

I brought you dragon bones.

I figure we can get weapons made for everyone.

I will work on it.

What is the timeline?

12 hours.

So kind of a rush job. I 'll make it happen.

See you then.

He poofs Alfheim.

I am here.

Frey show me what you have. 100000 Archer, 5 times that in swords, 20000 sorcerers and 10000 medics.

I will portal everyone to their places.

People start to line up in positions and groups.

Portals open and they appear as Set stands in the desert.

Why stand against Chaos you will lose.

I will fight for my rights.

As you are not part of the council I can't compel you to fight.

But I can send you somewhere, where you can't interfere. As the portal opens under him and he is gone.

Where you send him Calypso asks.

One place he can do no harm. Your Island.

My plants are going to be ruined.

Chapter 22

Incoming as a huge serpent flies over.

That is big.

Archers fire at will.

Levithan I summon you.

He takes to the sky to fight Aphosis.

Half of him resides in the water the other half in the sky.

He summons the Ageless to battle.

Chariots streak across the sky.

Lighting streaks across the sky.

He communicates telepathically to the other to hit the head and leave the body alone.

You puny mortals regardless of what you think.

The female Thor strikes him with her hammer and watches as he flies into the west. I might not kill you but you're going to hurt me when I am done with you and flies after the head hits him.

Zeus throws lightning bolts at him.

Arpthros throws webs around him, blinding the right eye.

As it turns red and burns away the web. You can't resist me.

Sir we need to regroup.

I have one more plan. He throws glass globes in his mouth and watches as he chomps down on them releasing gas that slowly turns him to stone.

He watches as he shifts forms. He appears as a tell human with shifty eyes and changing hair.

You only delay the end, I will have this planet just like I have taken the rest. I have been to the worlds you visited. All you do is murder and destroy everything. Without living beings there no need for Chaos,

I won't destroy you. I am just going to cause war and strife and let it fuel the Wheel of Chaos.

I want to introduce you to someone that is dead.

Sky released him.

Clement of the Azure Sky rises and faces the enemy.

Crystal Gaze.

Trying to turn me into a statue that is so original.

He steps out of the crystal form.

Like I said you defeat yourself if you want to be defeated.

The world needs Hades, I summon you.

Take him to a Godly prison in Tartarus.

I will put the serpent back to sleep in the depth of the oceans.

You just caused it to rise.

I am not done yet.

Only by defeating me can you win.

Your body is slowly turning to crystal.

Why your powers can keep it at bay.

You can defeat and hold off the crystal assault.

I figure one day you might beat it and I will have to deal with you then but enjoy your prison cell.

As Hades leads him away as I break the fortune token.

Fix the world and the battle damage let the world serpent the Ouroboro slumber.

Does the tapestry have a continuation.

Yes sir. Let us convene the council.

We have to prepare for his escape.

Why? The crystal virus won't hold long and based on the history it is a daily battle just to keep him from destroying this world. Why I have the power of the Sun God Ra his knowledge, his weapons, are lost in time. That the thing that can stand against him and truly cripple him.

Use the Eye.

I tried all four of them and nothing happened. Ra hid them somewhere and the Mantle forgot.

So what now?

Prepare for the next Cataclysm.

Fate keep an eye on the Tapestry and let me know of major events.

Epilogue

My kids stand as the Maiden of Honor and the Best Man as I wait for Calypso to walk down the aisle. As the room is decorated in blue and yellow. With flowers covering the arch. Music plays and she marches down the aisle to meet her soul mate. Ma'at pronounces them Titan and God. They poof to the Colorado hot springs for a relaxing night before the Dragon Academy opens.